Moki and the Magic Surfboard

A Hawaiian Fantasy

by Bruce Hale

With much aloha to all my good friends
(you know who you are)

Other Moki the Gecko books you may enjoy:

Legend of the Laughing Gecko
Surf Gecko to the Rescue!
The Adventures of Space Gecko
Moki the Gecko's Best Christmas Ever

Mahalo mucho to Hans Loffel, Brian Reed, Marie Miyashiro and Janette, as ever.

 For information, contact Words + Pictures Publishing, Inc., P.O. Box 61444, Honolulu, Hawaii 96839.

Library of Congress Catalog Card Number: 96-60743
ISBN: 0-9621280-5-8

4 6 8 10 9 7 5 3

Printed in Hong Kong.

Once upon a wave, Moki the Gecko was the finest surfer in all the islands. He could do barrel-rolls and spinners, fozzle-loops and fancy tricks like you've never seen before.

But that wasn't enough for Moki. He wanted to ride the biggest wave in the world — the biggest wave that ever curled.

Nobody believed he could. "Sure, anybody can do fancy tricks on a little board," said Kealii the Dolphin. "But if you try surfing such a monster wave, you'll be gecko sushi in a second."

Only his friend, Monk Seal, believed in Moki. "You can do it," she said. "But not on a normal board. You need a magic surfboard."

Now in those days, much like today, you couldn't just waltz over to the magic surfboard store and buy one off the rack. Only the *menehune*, a race of little people, had that kind of magic. But all the menehune had left the islands long ago, except one.

"And you never know what he'll do," said Monk Seal. "If the moon's in tune, and if you're lucky, and if he isn't in a bad mood, the Old Menehune just might make you a magic surfboard.

"But whatever you do," she said, "don't make him any promises. He's a sly one, that menehune."

One night when the Moon smiled a crooked crescent smile, Moki the Gecko waited on the wall beside the old menehune trail. Just before midnight, with a shuffling and a mumbling, came a white-bearded little man.

Moki jumped up and said, “I want to ask a favor — ” But before he could finish, the menehune had disappeared like sea foam on the sand.

"Wait!" cried the gecko. Only the wind replied. Moki pouted, "Hmph! Who needs you and your magic? I'll just use my own board."

The next morning, Moki paddled out from his favorite beach. The surf was big and getting bigger. He tried and tried to catch the mighty waves, but the gecko and his little board tumbled in the surf like twigs in a waterfall.

That night, Moki returned to the rock wall. Once again, the Old Menehune shuffled down the path. "Wait," called Moki. "Please, can you make me a magic surfboard?"

But once again, the Old Menehune vanished like an inkspot in the night.

Moki slumped against a tree. "Now how will I ever catch that wave?" he grumbled.

Just then, two bright menehune eyes peeked out around the tree trunk. Underneath them curled a wry, wrinkled menehune smile.

"A magic surfboard, eh?" chuckled the Old Menehune in his low, growly voice. "I could make you one. But first, you must promise me something: you must do me a favor in return, when I ask for it."

Moki stopped. He remembered Seal's warning about the sly menehune. But he'd never catch the world's biggest wave without a magic surfboard. "You've got a deal," the gecko sighed.

"Come back tomorrow night for your board," said the menehune.

Moki returned the following night. No surfboard. But the menehune sat and talked for hours about the ocean and the stars. Finally, Moki asked, “When will I get my surfboard?”

“Come again tomorrow,” said the menehune.

The next night, the moon was a little fuller and the menehune was a little more longwinded. He spun stories of his life among the moonlit mountains. And he made Moki tell him tales of surfing. Moki didn't mind it so much this time.

But when the menehune started telling his recipe for banana-and-dragonfly soup, Moki interrupted: "Look, it's not that I don't like talking with you, but will I ever get my magic surfboard?"

The menehune laughed. "Look behind the wall," he said. "You'll find your surfboard. But don't forget your promise."

Moki jumped over the wall and scooped it up off the grass — his own magic surfboard. It was covered with strange designs that glowed blue in the moonlight. When Moki turned to thank the menehune, the little man was gone.

At sunrise, Moki paddled far, far out to wait for the biggest wave. He waited three whole days. “I’m thirsty,” said Moki, and the magic surfboard gave him drink. “I’m hungry,” said Moki, and the magic surfboard gave him food.

It lulled him to sleep with lullabies at night.

Late on the third day, Moki heard a distant roar. Was it thunder? Was it a volcano? Was it a whale burp? No, it was the wave of a lifetime. Rising up from the ocean, taller than a mountain, came the biggest wave he had ever seen.

Moki told the magic surfboard, "Catch this wave." And sure enough, the board began to move. It caught the gigantic wave.

Moki looked down. He felt like he was riding on the clouds, the wave stretched so high. “Do some tricks,” he told the surfboard. And in a flash, the magic board spun and skipped, rolled and ripped, up and down and all around the huge wave.

Moki's loud gecko laugh rang out. "This is just like flying!" he giggled. No sooner had the words left his mouth, than the magic surfboard lifted off the wave and into the air.

Moki hung on with his sticky gecko feet, as the magic surfboard glided above the big wave, and...

..."Dive underwater!" he shouted. Splazoosh!! The magic surfboard dove far beneath the waves. Fabulous fish blinked in surprise at the surfing gecko speeding by.

"Up again," blurbled the gecko. And the magic surfboard rocketed up from the deep ocean, back onto the huge wave. Moki's imagination ran wild. What else could the magic board do?

“Can we go back in time?” he asked. In a blink, the air seemed to shimmy and shake. Moki found himself floating on the surfboard above an ancient world, filled with dinosaurs of all shapes and sizes.

"Howdy, cousin," said a brontosaurus. Moki the Gecko stopped for a picnic. The dinosaurs served him prehistoric bugs, like the harumphalos, which tastes just like chocolate cake, and the ruckaduckus, which lights up your belly on its way down. They played dinosaur games among the twisted trees.

Once, Moki thought he heard someone call his name. "That's funny," he said. "Nobody knows me here." He kept playing.

But as the prehistoric sun began to set, it was time to go. Moki waved good-bye, then stepped onto the magic surfboard and said, "Into the far future!"

In a flash, the air rippled again and the magic surfboard flew into a future stranger than any dream. People and animals lived in bubbles in the sky, drifting among clouds.

Moki landed the surfboard on a cloud bank. A troop of air lizards showed him how to bounce on the clouds like a huge feather bed.

Moki felt so comfortable. He settled into a cloud to sleep. But his sleep was troubled. The gecko dreamed that Monk Seal was saying something important, but Moki's ears were full of fluff.

Moki awoke. Again, he heard someone call his name, but could see no one. Then he remembered: the Old Menehune! "He must be in trouble," thought Moki. But the gecko wanted to stay and enjoy the future world.

What to do? While Moki stood and wondered, he heard his name called again. The gecko jumped onto his magic surfboard and said, “Find the menehune.”

Zip-zap-zoop! The surfboard returned him to his own time, floating right above a grass house. Below him, Moki heard humans.

One voice growled, “Make us some magic, you little runt — or else!” Through an open window, the gecko saw two big humans standing over the menehune, who was tied in ropes from head to foot like a sausage.

The Old Menehune said nothing. He just looked at Moki. And Moki knew: it was time to return his favor. The gecko thought fast. He could think of only one choice, and it was a hard one.

Finally, Moki whispered a command to the surfboard, then jumped onto the roof of the hut.

“Hoo-eeee!” yelled the gecko as loud as he could. “It’s a magic surfboard!” Two human heads poked out the window, and the surfboard spun gracefully through the air. It landed on the long grass.

“Grab it!” said one human. Both men burst from the hut. But just before they could reach the surfboard, it lifted off the grass and drifted further down the path. The men chased it, and all three soon disappeared into the woods.

Moki untied the menehune. "Took you long enough," grumbled the little man. "But never mind. You kept your promise, even if you lost the surfboard."

Moki sighed. "I didn't want to," he said. "Magic is so hard to find. But I couldn't leave you here."

The menehune laughed and clapped Moki on the back. "Little lizard," he said, "maybe someday you'll learn that the best kind of magic is found in friendship. Everything else is just hocus-pocus."

Moki didn't see what was so funny, but the Old Menehune kept laughing all the way to a high meadow, where he made them his famous banana-and-dragonfly soup.

And they drank every drop, and talked and watched the afternoon sun turn everything golden. Just like friends do.